LITTLENOSE THE MARKSMAN

Littlenose's spear throwing might have been a joke if it hadn't been so dangerous. All he had to do was appear at the entrance to the family cave carrying his boy-sized spear, and the members of the tribe vanished like frightened rabbits.

Father felt it was a terrible disgrace and something must be done . . .

Littlenose was invented for John Grant's own children, but was soon entertaining millions more when he first appeared on Jackanory in 1968.

The Neanderthal boy whose pet was bought in a mammoth sale, whose mother is in despair at the rough treatment he gives his furs, and whose exasperated father sometimes threatens to feed him to a sabre-toothed tiger, is everybody's favourite.

Besides gaining wide acceptance in Great Britain, the Littlenose stories have been translated into German, French, Italian, Spanish and Japanese.

LITTLENOSE THE MARKSMAN

John Grant

Illustrated by the author

BBC/KNIGHT

Copyright © John Grant 1982
First published 1982 by British
Broadcasting Corporation/
Knight Books
Seventh impression 1987

Printed and bound in Great
Britain for the British Broadcasting
Corporation, 35 Marylebone High
Street, London W1M 4AA and
Hodder and Stoughton
Paperbacks, a division of Hodder
and Stoughton Ltd., Mill Road,
Dunton Green, Sevenoaks, Kent
(Editorial Office: 47 Bedford
Square, London, WC1 3DP) by
Richard Clay Ltd., Bungay,
Suffolk.

British Library C.I.P.

Grant, John
    Littlenose the marksman.
    I. Title
    823'.914[J]   PZ7

    ISBN 0-340-28653-9
        (0-563-20083-9 BBC)

Contents

Littlenose the Marksman

Neanderthal men had to be good spear throwers. Accurate spear throwing could mean the difference between supper for a hunter's family – or supper for someone else's, like a sabre-toothed tiger's. Because of this, most hunters were very good at throwing spears, and some were brilliant. Father was one of these (as he never stopped telling Littlenose), and he felt that it was a terrible disgrace that Littlenose was probably the worst spear thrower who had ever lived.

Littlenose's spear throwing might have been a joke, if it hadn't been so dangerous. All he had to do was appear at the entrance to the family cave carrying his boy-size spear, and the members of the tribe vanished like rabbits. It wasn't that Littlenose didn't practise. He went to lessons with the other Neanderthal boys, and practised each night while Father shouted encouragement . . . and a lot of other things. But he still couldn't throw a spear properly.

One night, just as they were finishing supper, Father said, "I've made up my mind. We're going to end this spear nonsense once and for all. Tomorrow I am taking you out to practise, and we are not coming home until you can get it right. In fact, we will start now, before you go to bed."

So, while Mother cleared up the supper things, Father fetched his spear and gave Littlenose a lecture on the finer points of the art. Not that Littlenose needed the lecture; he could have given it himself, so many times had he heard it.

"The weight goes on the right foot," began Father. "Shoulders square. Spear gripped firmly but lightly. Think of it as part of your arm. Eye on target. Smooth swing and follow-through."

And Littlenose did all of these things, without of course actually letting go of the spear.

Father beamed. "Lovely, lovely!" he cried. "What a beautiful action! You're taking after me at last. Do that tomorrow, and you'll be junior champion of the tribe."

Littlenose shrugged his shoulders. What a waste of time, spending tomorrow chucking a rotten old spear about when he could be having fun with Two-Eyes. However, he carried on practising until bedtime, and fell asleep sure that his arm was going to fall off.

Next morning, after breakfast, Father got ready for Littlenose's lesson. Littlenose picked up the

spear and stood near the cave entrance to wait.
Might as well try a few loosening-up exercises, he
thought. He held the spear firmly but lightly, weight
on his right foot, and went through the smooth
swing and follow-through action. And he forgot to
hold on to the spear. It sailed out of the cave and
straight through a pair of best furs hung out to dry
by a neighbour. Naturally there was some
unpleasantness, ending with the neighbour
shouting, ". . . and take that boy of yours as far
away as you can. And if you never bring him back it
will be too soon!"

"That's another fine mess you've got me into,"
grumbled Father, as they went into the forest. They
walked a long way, until they came to a clearing, at
the edge of which stood a tall tree. During the winter
gales a big branch had broken off and left a scar on
the trunk. The scar formed a circle with rings, and
Father pointed at it. "That," he explained, "is your
target." He walked to the opposite edge of the
clearing and scored a mark on the ground with his
spear. "Stand here," he said, "and try to stick the
spear in the centre of the circle. Like this." And
without even taking particular aim, or so it seemed
to Littlenose, he threw the spear so that it stuck,
quivering, right in the centre of the target. "Now,
you try," said Father.

Littlenose held the spear firmly but lightly, and
threw the spear exactly as he had practised the

evening before. The spear whizzed through the air
. . . and stuck in the tree about three hand widths
above the target.

"A bit high," said Father. "Try again." This time
the spear stuck in about three hand widths *below* the
target.

"Now," said Father, "right in the middle this
time." The spear hit a branch off to the left. Then to
the right. Then down to the left. And up to the right.
Everywhere but on the target.

And so it went on. When the sun was high in the
sky, Father was almost weeping with vexation, and
the only mark on the target was the spot where
Father had hit it. All around, however, was
peppered with spear-holes from Littlenose's
unsuccessful efforts.

Father looked at the sun. It was almost midday.

"Have one more go," he said, wearily. "Then we'll go home for lunch. Let's see if we can tell Mother that at least you hit the *target* once, if not actually in the middle."

Littlenose sighed, gripped the spear in the correct manner, kept his eye on the target – and missed the tree altogether.

Father jumped up and down. "I don't believe it," he cried. "How could any son of mine be so stupid? Go and fetch the spear, and we'll go home." For the first time that day, Littlenose began to feel faintly cheerful. He trotted round the tree and behind the bushes which grew at its foot. But there was no spear. "I can't find it," he called.

Father joined him. "It must be somewhere," he said, impatiently. "You just haven't *looked* properly." But, he couldn't find it either. Father and Littlenose poked about among the bushes and in the long grass . . . but, no spear.

"We might as well just go home," said Littlenose. "It's only an old spear."

"What do you mean? Old spear?" shouted Father. "It was one of my best!" And he began rummaging about among the bushes again. Littlenose had already lost what little interest he had in the problem of the lost spear and had wandered away a short distance. Suddenly he stopped, and called, "I think I know where it went. I think it's in *there*." And he pointed to a hollow tree trunk lying half-hidden in the long grass.

"Well, don't just stand there," said Father. "Get it out."

Littlenose made a face. "You don't think I'm crawling in there?" he exclaimed. "It's dark and damp and smelly, and I bet it's full of spiders and earwigs and creepy-crawlies that go in your hair and inside your furs."

Father gave him a look. "Hmph!" he said. "I suppose I'll have to get it myself, like everything else in this family." He got down on all fours and began to grope his way inside the hollow trunk. It was a tight squeeze, and Littlenose watched as Father's head, then his shoulders, then the rest of his body vanished from sight. He stood scuffing his feet in the long grass, and Father's knees were just disappearing when he kicked something hard. He bent down. "Father," he called, "I've found the spear! You can come out."

And Father's voice, sounding rather odd, echoed from inside the tree: "I CAN'T! I'M STUCK!"

Littlenose looked in amazement. All that could be seen of Father were his feet sticking out of one end of the log. "Can't you get out at all?" said Littlenose.

The noise that came from the log made Littlenose jump back. "In that case," he said, "I'd better get you out." He gripped Father's ankles, leaned back, and heaved.

"STOP! STOP!" screamed Father. "You're pulling my ears off!"

Littlenose let go, and walked round to the other end of the hollow log. "I'll try pushing," he said. "That ought to work." He sat down with his legs inside the tree and his feet against the top of Father's head. Then he took a firm hold of the tree and pushed. "STOP!" yelled Father again. "You're taking my nose off!"

"Well, there's nothing for it," said Littlenose. "I'll have to get help. Perhaps if Mother boiled up some bear grease and poured it . . ."

But Father interrupted in a panic-stricken voice: "You can't leave me like this," he cried. "I'm helpless. Anything might come along and bite me!"

"There might be a way," said Littlenose, thoughtfully. "If I pushed a bit, and pulled a bit, and used the spear as a lever, and you sort of kicked your feet . . . do you think you might be able to stand up?"

It took much more pulling, pushing, levering and kicking than Littlenose had imagined, but at length Father managed to lurch unsteadily to his feet. And Littlenose burst out laughing.

"What's so funny?" said Father hollowly through

a narrow crack in the trunk.

"Nothing, really," said Littlenose, trying to keep his face straight. "It's just that I've never seen a tree with feet before."

"Well, stop messing about, and get me home," said Father.

"Right," said Littlenose. "Follow me." And he strode off in the direction of the caves.

Father tottered for a few steps, banged into a tree and wandered round in a circle before he called: "I can't follow you! I can hardly see a thing through the crack."

"Oh, all right," said Littlenose patiently, "take my hand."

"How can I take your hand?" said Father. "My arms are stuck inside this thing with me!"

"Don't worry," said Littlenose. "I'll take your branch."

"You'll what?" said a mystified Father.

Littlenose didn't bother to try to explain. He reached up and got hold of a branch still attached to the dead tree and began to lead Father in the direction of home, where he was sure Mother would know how to get Father out, probably, he still thought, by using boiling bear fat.

They made good progress, with only the occasional yell from Father as Littlenose accidentally led him through a patch of nettles or over a sharp stone. Then Littlenose was suddenly

almost jerked off his feet as Father came to an
abrupt halt. The dead tree swayed about, while a
wheezy voice panted through the crack: "I – can't –
go – another – step! I'm – exhausted! It isn't – every
– day – that – I – carry – trees – around – the – forest
– like – this!"

"We're almost there," said Littlenose, encouragingly.

"You – go – on – and – fetch – Mother –" gasped Father. "I'll – wait – here."

"Not here, you can't," said Littlenose. You're right in the middle of the path! People won't be able to get past. I'll guide you to one side." He took Father's branch again and moved him to one side. "He makes quite a handsome tree," thought Littlenose, as he looked back before running as fast as he could to fetch Mother.

As Littlenose's footsteps faded in the distance,
Father began to get his breath back. He found that if
he bent his knees the trunk took its own weight
against the ground and he could rest. It wasn't too
uncomfortable, and he began to relax, closed his
eyes, and fell asleep.

Father woke with the sound of voices. He twisted
round and managed to get an eye to the crack in the
trunk. And saw a most alarming sight!

Coming through the woods towards him was a
couple of Neanderthal hunters. But they weren't
carrying spears. They were carrying big stone axes
and were talking in loud voices.

"No, green wood's no good for fires. It just fills your cave with smoke."

"Quite right. Dead wood's best. But where can you find a dead tree nowadays? They've all been cut down years ago."

"Yes, I can remember when I was a lad, you could . . . wait a minute! What's that?"

"It's a . . . a . . . dead tree."

"Where did it come from?"

"Don't be daft, they don't come from anywhere. They grow."

"But it wasn't here yesterday! And as far as I remember it's only mushrooms that grow in a night. Not trees. Especially dead ones."

"Perhaps it's magic!"

"Magic or no magic, it's good fire wood, and I'm going to cut it down."

The man stepped forward and swung his axe back.

"OH, NO YOU'RE NOT!" shouted a strange voice from the tree.

At that moment Mother and Littlenose came out from among the trees and saw an incredible sight. In one direction a pair of brawny Neanderthal hunters were throwing away their axes, running for their lives, and screaming in terror. And, in the opposite direction a tree was running . . . also screaming in terror.

Mother and Littlenose ran as fast as they could. "It's all right, Father," shouted Littlenose. "We won't let anyone cut you down."

But Father was too terrified to listen. He burst out from among the trees right in front of the caves, where the rest of the tribe were preparing to have lunch. A tree bewitched, they thought. A thousand times worse than even Littlenose and his spear. In a moment, every cooking fire had been abandoned and the tribe watched fearfully from their caves as Father ran round and round.

Then, quite abruptly, Father's strength gave out. As Mother and Littlenose came out of the forest they saw him come to a sudden stop, sway to and fro for a moment, then down he crashed in a great shower of rotten wood, bark, spiders, earwigs and creepy-crawlies as the tree trunk burst into a thousand pieces, and left Father lying on the ground wondering if it were the end of the world.

The tribe looked on as Littlenose helped him to his feet. "Stupid game to play at his age! You can see where that boy of his takes it all from," they said.

Mother fetched a pot of bear grease to rub on Father's bruises. (Littlenose knew she'd use it for something.) And Littlenose didn't bother to ask if they were going to do more spear-throwing in the afternoon. He was already planning a super game to play with Two-Eyes after lunch.

Littlenose the Horseman

The Neanderthal folk loved horses. They also loved apples, honey and nuts. Horse flesh for the Neanderthal folk was good eating, while horses' skins provided first-class leather for belts and bags and things. But, there was a problem. Horses were difficult to catch. It wasn't that they ate people, like black bears, or were fierce like forest cattle. It was just that they were very intelligent. One horse was brighter than ten Neanderthal hunters any day.

Littlenose had only once been on a horse hunt, and while he had plenty of adventures, none of them had anything to do with horses. THAT part had been incredibly boring. And so, when a horse hunt was announced Littlenose hoped that he *wouldn't* be among the apprentice hunters chosen to accompany the grown-ups. But, his luck was out. He came home muttering and mumbling to himself. Father also came home muttering . . . but not to himself.

"A horse hunt is bad enough," he said. "But with Littlenose! Oh, dear! It doesn't bear thinking about!" And he set about getting his hunting gear ready for the morning.

The hunting party assembled at dawn in front of the caves. Nobody spoke. They just looked at the ground and shuffled their feet in gloomy silence. Even Littlenose was depressed.

Suddenly, the silence was broken by a cheery shout. "Hello, there! I'm not too late to join in, am I?"

"Uncle Redhead!" shouted Littlenose.

"That's *all* we need," said Father.

"We can't wait," said the Chief Hunter. "We're just leaving.

"That's all right," said Uncle Redhead. "I've got everything I need. Be prepared! That's my motto." And he pointed to the pack he carried on his back. "In fact, I've brought along a handy gadget which might just come in useful. Saw a chap using it on an elk hunt last week. Very impressive."

"More gimmicks," grumbled Father. "Why can't people be content to hunt the way nature intended?"

25

A moment later the order was given to march. And the other hunters seemed quite glad to have Uncle Redhead. Up through the woods the hunters went and out on to the high moor. There they stopped and gathered around Nosey, the Chief Tracker. Nosey turned this way and that, twitching his large and handsome nose as he sniffed and snuffed at the breeze. Then he got down on all fours and snuffled about among the grass and stones. Finally, he stood up and pointed towards the horizon. "That way," he said. "They passed at dawn, a large herd, travelling fast."

"In that case, we had better do the same," said the Chief Hunter; and they set off in pursuit.

All day the hunting party trudged along. They stopped briefly to eat at midday, then went on. The moor remained empty. There was nothing to be seen, and the hunters shuffled along, trying to think beautiful thoughts to ease their boredom. It was a typical horse hunt.

Suddenly, Nosey held up his hand and said: "STOP!" He spoke so suddenly that the hunters bumped into each other, and waited in a bad-tempered huddle for Nosey to speak again. They were at the foot of a long ridge which cut off the view in front.

"Beyond that ridge," said Nosey in a whisper, "is a large herd of horses."

"How do you know?" asked someone.

"We trackers KNOW these things," said Nosey in a slightly huffy tone of voice.

"All right, all right," said the Chief Hunter. "But we'd better make sure all the same. Hi, Littlenose, up on the ridge with you and see what's what!"

Littlenose laid down his spear and crept cautiously towards the skyline. At the top he gently parted the long grass and peered into the distance. He didn't have to peer very far. Half a dozen spear shots away a big herd of the small shaggy Ice Age horses was grazing quietly, raising their heads from

time to time to sniff the breeze. Their long tails and manes ruffled in the wind, and they were close enough for Littlenose to make out their spotted markings.

Now, while the Neanderthal hunting party had been following in the wake of the horses, hunters of a completely different kind had also selected the herd as an item on the menu. A family of permanently hungry and half-mad hyenas who lived on the edge of the moor had set off long before Littlenose and the others. They went loping across the moor in their own ungainly fashion, laughing crazily among themselves from time to time. Like the Neanderthal hunters they hoped to catch a stray horse which had separated from the herd. But, instead of following the horses and trusting to luck, the hyenas planned to scare the herd into a stampede and grab a horse in the confusion. So, while Littlenose made his report, the hyenas were already in position, waiting for the right moment.

The hunters gathered around the Chief Hunter, and he had just started to say, "This is how we'll do it . . ." when Littlenose cried: "What's that!"

There was a loud drumming in the air and a throbbing in the ground beneath their feet.

"It's the horses," cried Littlenose. "Stampeding! RUN FOR YOUR LIVES!"

The hyenas had chosen their moment, and charged. The horses raced in panic up and over the ridge, right on top of the hunters. The hunters screamed and shrieked in terror, so that the horses shied away and wheeled round in the direction of the hyenas who fled as fast as their legs would carry them to avoid being trampled.

By the time that the noise died in the distance and the dust had settled it was growing dark. There was nothing more the Neanderthal hunters could do but make camp for the night.

They didn't sleep much. Apart from the bumps
and bruises you would expect from being trampled
on by a herd of wild horses, the hyenas sat on a
nearby knoll and chuckled the night away. "It's all
their fault," grumbled Father at breakfast.

"Actually," said Uncle Redhead, "they've given
me an idea. After all, they did drive the horses
towards us, and if we'd been ready we could have
had them. I think we should try the same thing
again, but more organised this time."

"You got a tame hyena with you?" asked Father
sarcastically.

"No," said Uncle Redhead, "but half of us could
drive the horses towards the other half of the party.
All we have to do is find out where they've gone."

31

This was another job for Nosey's wonderful nose. For another day the hunters trailed behind him until late in the afternoon they came out of a thin straggle of trees . . . and there, at last, were the horses again. A wide, deep gulley led down into a hollow where the herd was grazing. Bushes grew along the bottom and up the sides of the gulley.

"Now," said Uncle Redhead, "if we drive them up the gulley, it should be easy enough to catch at least one as they gallop through the bushes."

"How?" asked Father.

"With my gadget," said Uncle Redhead. He reached into his pack and pulled out a coil of raw-hide rope. "I'll be waiting," he said. "All you lot have to do is drive the horses up the gulley."

The rest of the hunters looked amazed. "You expect to catch a horse with THAT?" one of them asked.

"Just wait," said Uncle Redhead. "Just wait."

With Littlenose and one or two others, Uncle Redhead took up his position near the top of the gulley, rope in one hand, while the rest of the hunters circled round the hollow. Then they started driving the horses. They shouted and clapped. They rattled spears together. And the horses stampeded, racing out of the hollow in a great cloud of dust.

"Here they come," shouted Littlenose. Uncle Redhead took the end of the rope in one hand and began to whirl it around his head. As he whirled the

rope it opened out into a wide loop. The first horses
were breaking out through the bushes, and the dust
was blinding, but still Uncle Redhead stood,
whirling the rope round his head.

Then he threw it . . . right into the thickest part of
the dust cloud, where judging by the noise of
crashing in the bushes, a very large horse was
making its escape. The rope went suddenly taut,
and Uncle Redhead shouted, "Help me! I've a big
one! Pull it off its feet!"

Littlenose and the others quickly grabbed hold of the rope which seemed about to drag Uncle Redhead along after the horses. The rope jumped and jerked, but slowly and surely something very heavy and extremely active was being dragged out of the bushes. It was also something very noisy. In a rather surprising way. Littlenose knew that horses neigh, whinny and even squeal. But this horse was *shouting*! And not very nice things at that, as the hunters dragged to the side of the gulley not a horse, but a scratched, dusty and irate . . . FATHER!

He struggled to his feet, his arms pinned to his sides by the rope, and his face purple with rage. He charged at Uncle Redhead. "Get this thing off me," he raged. Uncle Redhead didn't think that such a good idea in the circumstances, but he ran to the farthest loose end of the rope and gave it a twitch so that the loop came loose and fell at Father's feet.

It took the best part of that day and most of the night to pacify Father. Then they discussed their next move. They would give the new method one more try . . . but *without* the benefit of Uncle Redhead's rope. "A spear was good enough for our fathers, and theirs before that," declared the hunters.

It was afternoon before they spotted the horses again, and crept as close as they could. Nearby was the remains of an ancient forest, bent and twisted from the gales of many Ice Age winters. The trees would provide cover for the hunters as the horses were driven towards them. The driving party set off at once to get behind the herd, and this time Father stayed with the others. He was taking no chances!

Littlenose waited impatiently for the hunt to start. There was no sign as yet of stampeding horses, and he strained his eyes for the first glimpse of action. Then he had a better idea. Why not climb one of the trees and get a proper view? He was just settled comfortably on a branch when he heard distant shouts and the thunder of many hooves. The horses scattered in all directions, but most of them galloped straight for the trees. This was exciting. The hunters gripped their spears . . .

Under the trees swept the panicking horses. Any moment now the long hunt would have been all worth while. Then something fell out of the sky! The leading horse gave a terrified squeal and bolted in a totally unexpected direction. The hunters were too surprised to do anything, and for a moment horses and hunters milled around each other, bumping and jostling, until the horses were clear of the trees and disappearing in a cloud of dust . . . and Littlenose went with them! Too late he had remembered he should hold on, then he was falling. He bounced once, twice, on something hard and hairy, and was then whirled away as fast as the wind, clinging to the mane of a startled horse and desperately trying not to be battered against the hard ground.

Astonished, the hunters watched the horse race and buck, trying to get rid of its unwelcome passenger. Then it stretched out its neck and

galloped straight across the moor.

"Well, there goes Littlenose," cried someone as the horse vanished into the distance.

"And here he comes again," cried someone else as the horse reappeared going even faster than before.

"That's my boy," said Father excitedly. "Hunting with his bare hands. Takes after me, of course!"

Littlenose didn't know whether he was more afraid of falling off or being carried away. He managed to haul himself astride the horse, wrapping his arms around the animal's neck. He wondered if horses tired easily. It seemed his only hope.

Six times he charged past the hunters, and each time they cheered louder than before.

And of course, the horse was as anxious to be rid
of Littlenose as Littlenose was to be rid of *him*. It
was more intelligent than ten Neanderthal hunters,
let alone apprentices, and as it galloped it racked its
brain to think of some way.

Ah, yes! Of course! The horse suddenly wheeled
off in a new direction. Faster and faster. Its hooves
barely touched the ground.

Then it stopped. It sat back on its haunches and
skidded along the ground, its hooves sending the
turf flying in all directions. Littlenose flew straight
between its ears and over its head . . . and landed in
the middle of the weediest, slimiest pond he had
ever seen. The horse stood on the bank for a
moment, then with a neigh that sounded very like a
laugh, it turned, arched its neck, tossed its tail and
cantered off.

The hunters found Littlenose sitting on the bank scraping off mud.

"What a performance," cried Uncle Redhead. "This is something to think about. All we have to do is tame a few horses and there's no limit to where a man might travel."

Father laughed. "It'll never catch on," he said.

As he set off with the others on the trek home, for once Littlenose agreed with him.

Littlenose the Artist

Uncle Redhead was staying for a few days with
Littlenose and his family, and one evening the talk
around the fire was about the Straightnoses, and in
particular their fantastic success as hunters.

"They cheat, of course," said Father, firmly. "All
that magic of theirs. Painting pictures on rocks.
Singing and dancing in front of them. It's not
natural! No good will come of it; mark my words!"

"I do, dear, I do," said Mother. "But they still
catch more animals than you!"

Father gave her a look, but Uncle Redhead broke
in: "There's no such thing as magic. They're just
better hunters. That's all."

"But what about all that painted cave stuff, and
the singing and dancing?" said Father. "Don't tell
me that they don't do that for a good reason."

"For the best possible reason," said Uncle Redhead. "To have a good time. Their real secret is that they don't spend their lives stuck in caves, like you lot do. They are on the move the whole time, *following* the animal herds instead of just waiting for them to turn up when they want meat. Maybe the Neanderthal folk should do the same."

"The very idea!" exclaimed Mother. "That's just not respectable; and that's no way to speak in front of a child. I hope Littlenose didn't hear."

But Littlenose *had* heard. He was sitting some distance apart playing a game with twigs and stones, and had listened with great interest to the whole conversation. Uncle Redhead, he knew, was the cleverest person in the whole world, but surely this time he had got it wrong. There must be magic in the painted rocks, and the more Littlenose thought about it the more a marvellous idea grew in his mind. He would try it himself! He would make some paintings of his own, and see if he could magic up some game as the Straightnoses did.

42

First he had to make some paint. He collected as many different colours of clay, earth, juice and soft stone as he could find. Then he mixed them with water in an old piece of clay pot. What sort of animal should he paint? What sort of animal *could* he paint? After all, he had never painted anything in his life before.

With a fistful of dry grass, Littlenose began daubing at the wall of the cave above his bed. Black. Brown. White. Ochre. Grey. He smeared it. He smudged it, mixed it, dabbed it with his fingers, and stood back to admire his handiwork. It didn't look much like any animal he could remember . . . but it did bear some sort of resemblance to . . . to . . . to Mother!

The next moment Littlenose was cowering back on his bed while Mother, whom he had thought safely at the river fetching water, shrieked at him: "LITTLENOSE! Get this mess cleaned up! Just look at the wall. *And* it's on the bed-clothes!"

Littlenose blinked up at her in astonishment. It had WORKED! He had painted a picture of Mother, and here she was, magicked from the river bank in the twinkling of an eye! "It's magic!" he stammered.

"You'll need more than magic if Father sees this mess," said Mother. And Littlenose reluctantly set to work scraping his masterpiece off the wall. As he scraped, he thought, "It might just have been chance, but I don't think so. I'll try again, but somewhere where I won't get into bother for making a mess."

He would need plenty of paint if he were to portray one of the larger animals, so he borrowed a large clay pot when Mother wasn't looking. He decided on only one colour this time . . . brown. It would be less trouble, and most animals were some sort of brown anyway. He found some sticky, brown clay by the river and put several handfuls into the pot. To make sure that the paint would stick properly, he added handfuls of mashed-up sticky berries and even sacrificed a piece of honeycomb he got from a neighbour for running an errand. Then, with a long stick, he began to stir the strange-looking mixture.

It was hard work, and after a lot of effort the paint was still very runny with lumps. His arms were aching, and it was almost suppertime, so he hid the pot of paint and went home. Mother was about to serve the boiled woolly rhinoceros and was just giving it a last stir before she lifted the pot from the fire.

The fire! That was the secret!

Mother mixed all sorts of things in a pot, and they always turned out right because she put the pot on the fire. If he did the same the problem of the lumpy paint would be solved. There was, however, a snag. Mother was unlikely to take kindly to the sight of one of her pots simmering on the fire with a mixture of clay and sticky berries. It looked as if he would have to make his own fire in the forest somewhere.

Next day, at breakfast, his luck changed. Father left early to go for a morning's fishing with two friends, and Mother had just cleared away the breakfast things when a neighbour hurried in. Her old mother was sick. Could Mother look after her twins, just for the morning? Mother said she would and hurried off, leaving Littlenose on his own. Now was his chance!

Littlenose fetched the clay pot with its curious mixture from its hiding place and balanced it on the stones around the fire. Then he started stirring. He stirred and stirred while the sweat dripped from his forehead, but the paint looked and felt much as it had done before, except that it was now bubbling and giving off wisps of steam.

Littlenose was so hot that he decided that the pot could get on with it by itself while he went outside to cool off. He walked down to the river and sat on the bank. It was cool, and the ripples made a very restful pattern on the water. So restful that Littlenose fell asleep.

He woke with a start, and tried to think what he
had been doing. Then he remembered the pot. It
was still on the fire. How long had he been asleep?
Mother might be on her way home even now! He
ran as fast as he could to the cave, but all was well.
The fire had died down a bit, but the pot was still
bubbling gently. He was just wondering how he
could lift the pot from the fire without burning his
fingers, when he heard voices. Not Mother. No.
Much worse! It was Father, and he'd brought his
two fishing companions with him. Littlenose dived
to the back of the cave and buried himself under his
fur bed-covers. Would Father notice the pot
bubbling and steaming on the fire?

He heard the men put down their fishing gear, then Father's voice said, "My wife and boy seem to be out, but I see they've left lunch ready. We're very organised in this cave, you know."

"What on earth is he talking about?" thought Littlenose. "Lunch?"

Then he heard Father again: "Grab a bowl and help yourselves. My wife's a wonderful cook; this is something you won't forget in a hurry, I promise you."

Littlenose carefully raised the bed-clothes. It was horrible! Father and the men were sitting around the fire with clay bowls, taking turns with a bone ladle to scoop the lumpy brown liquid from Littlenose's pot. Then, one of them lifted the bowl to his lips and took a mouthful. Littlenose couldn't look. He closed his eyes.

Nothing happened for a moment, then with a strangled yell the man dropped the bowl and ran out of the cave.

"Funny chap," said Father. "Not too hot, is it?"
And he also took a mouthful. Littlenose couldn't
remember anything more awful. Father ran round
and round the cave, spitting paint all over the floor
and shouting: "POISON! I'VE BEEN
POISONED!"

The second man wisely put his bowl on the floor
untasted, and started banging Father on the back in
a well-meaning sort of way. Eventually, after a drink
of water Father recovered somewhat. He was still a
funny colour, and when his friend suggested that
some fresh air might help, he staggered outside.

This was Littlenose's chance. Wrapping his hands in some old scraps of fur he lifted the pot from the fire and carried it out of the cave and into the forest. Then he dashed back inside and cleaned out the bowls, mopped up the floor, and generally removed all traces of the disaster. And when Mother came home she didn't understand what Father was talking about; so that even he began to wonder if it had all been a bad dream.

So at last, Littlenose had his paint. Not very good paint, perhaps, but it would have to do. Early next morning he set off, staggering under the weight of the paint pot to find a suitable rock. And, in a clearing he found just what he wanted, a great pile of boulders. One of those would do admirably.

He put the pot on the ground and walked around the rock pile. What he really needed was a flat slab, but these were all rounded and covered with moss. On the second time round he paused, then took a step back and had another look. Yes! It was unmistakable. From a distance the mossy boulders looked like a large animal. A large woolly animal. But what, exactly? Well, nothing *exactly*, but Littlenose thought that with a little help it could become something quite convincing. And, what's more, probably even more magic than an ordinary rock painting.

He climbed on to the rocks and began to clean off some of the moss. Then he pulled out some tufts of grass. The hardest job was a small bush growing on top. He broke off the twigs and leaves so that only two large stems remained. Those he broke short before stripping the bark to leave them gleaming white. He didn't require much paint; just enough to make a pair of eyes, two nostrils, and a mouth. Pieces of bark wedged into a crack became ears . . . and there it was! A woolly rhinoceros!

"If that doesn't work," thought Littlenose, "nothing will."

He planned to return to the clearing next day to put it to the test, but to his disgust he discovered he was to accompany a grown-up hunting party. That was the worst of being an apprentice hunter! They set off through the early-morning damp of the forest,

keeping a sharp look-out for animal tracks.
Littlenose muttered to himself that the whole thing
was a waste of time, and it looked as if he were
probably right. There was neither sight nor sound of
a single huntable animal. The Chief Hunter ordered
a rest, while one man was sent on ahead to see if it
were worth going on. He was back in a few
moments, running, gasping for breath, and almost
speechless with excitement.

"Over there," he gasped. "The biggest I've ever seen! A rhinoceros! In a clearing. Lurking in the long grass."

"It didn't see you? Didn't move?"

"No," said the man, "it just lurked."

"What do you think, men?" said the Chief Hunter.

A woolly rhinoceros was something a Neanderthal hunter avoided, if at all possible . . . particularly if it was the biggest ever seen. "Why not?" said one of the hunters, and in a moment the whole party was hurrying towards the clearing. Only Littlenose hung back, trying to look invisible. He was sure something awful was about to happen . . . and he would get all the blame.

The hunters reached the edge of the clearing. They saw two long horns, gleaming white in the sun. As the man had said, it didn't move, it just lurked. There was a short, whispered discussion, then Father stepped forward, spear at the ready. It was brand new. This would put it to the test. He gave a loud yell and hurled the spear. It was a beautiful shot. It hit the rhino right between the eyes . . . and shattered into a thousand pieces!

"I knew they were tough," he said, "but this is ridiculous!" He took a long look at the rhino. "Someone," he said, "has been playing the fool!"

Littlenose began to slip away. He stopped. Something was coming. Something that crashed through the trees and shook the ground beneath it. "RUN!" he shouted. "RUN!"

The hunting party fled in all directions as a
REAL woolly rhinoceros burst into view. "It's
worked again," thought Littlenose.

But, magic or not, the rhino had no eyes for the
fleeing Neanderthal men. Its beady little eyes were
firmly fixed on the other rhinoceros which had
trespassed on to its territory. It darted out from the
trees and met the intruder head on with a sound like
a thunderclap. Pieces of rock flew in all directions as
the startled animal bounced back on to its haunches
with an earth-shaking thump. For a moment it
might have been an easy target, but the hunters
were as astonished as the rhino at the turn of events.

Before anyone could move, it staggered to its feet and tottered in a bemused fashion back into the forest.

The hunters, particularly Father, looked at the broken spear, the paint-smeared rocks, and finally at Littlenose.

And Littlenose made up his mind there and then that magic was just too tricky to handle. If the Straightnoses DID use magic then they must be even cleverer than people thought. Magic just brought trouble. But troubles didn't usually last for ever, and with that comforting thought, Littlenose shouldered his spear and trudged off behind the others on the long trek home.

Littlenose's Hibernation

It had been snowing all night; come to think of it, it had been snowing all *week*. The Ice Age landscape was covered in snow . . . and ice, of course. In the caves of the Neanderthal folk snores came from under fur bed-clothes, while the sun rose reluctantly over the trees, its pale winter light shining into the caves to tell people that it was time to get up.

Littlenose poked his berry-sized nose out of the covers, and quickly pulled it back again. He screwed up his eyes and shivered. "If I had *my* way," he thought, "no one would get up at this time of year. Everyone would stay in bed until spring." He pulled the covers closer around his ears, but only succeeded in letting in a cold draught.

The cold draught was nothing to the icy blast which hit him as Father dragged the covers off. "Up you get," he shouted. "You can't lie there all day. There's work to be done. We're out of firewood, and Mother needs water from the river before she can make breakfast."

Pulling on his winter furs, Littlenose left the cave and trudged through the snow towards the river, a clay pot on his shoulder and a stone axe in his hand. "Fill that pot! Chop that wood! That's all I ever hear these days," he muttered to himself.

He muttered while he broke a hole in the river ice with the axe and filled the pot with water. He was still muttering as he brought it back to the cave, and he continued to mutter as he chopped a branch from a dead tree and dragged it home. "Stop muttering," said Mother. "I think you must have got out of bed on the wrong side this morning."

"If I had my way," thought Littlenose to himself, "I wouldn't have got out of *any* side of the bed at all."

Over breakfast, he continued to think: people were stupid. Birds and animals had more sense. The elk had left months ago for warmer places to spend the winter; and the wild geese had flown far away to the south where it was always summer. The last course for breakfast was a few hazel nuts. Littlenose crouched close to the fire to eat them. "Squirrels eat nuts," he said to himself. "They collect them in the autumn, and only get up to eat one or two if they wake up feeling peckish. They sleep more or less all winter. I wish I could do the same."

Suddenly, he jumped up, scattering nuts all over the floor. Why *couldn't* he sleep all winter, hibernate like the squirrels and the bears and the dormice? But it was not something to be done on the spur of the moment. It required a lot of thought.

That night after supper, Father sat with an air of great concentration binding a new flint point on to his spear, and Mother was sewing. Littlenose hesitated for a moment, then spoke to Mother. "I'm going to hibernate," he said.

"Well, do it quietly, dear," said Mother, without looking up. "Don't disturb Father. You know what he's like when he's busy."

Littlenose started to say something, but decided not to. He *had* tried to tell them about his intentions, and it shouldn't come as too much of a shock.

The shock was Littlenose's next morning. When Father as usual pulled the covers off him, Littlenose pulled them right back on again. "I'm hibernating," he said, eyes shut tight. Next moment he was standing shivering outside the cave where Father had yanked him by one ear. His winter furs landed at his feet, and Father shouted, "Get dressed, and stop this nonsense! There's work to do."

As he did his morning water and firewood fetching, Littlenose muttered more than usual, but he had to admit to himself that he had handled the whole scheme very badly. The problem was that the cave wasn't his, it was Father's. And Father made the rules. Bears and other hibernators prepared special places to spend the winter. He would have to do the same.

As soon as Father and Mother were busy, Littlenose slipped into his own special corner of the cave and gathered up his bedding, plus a few fur rugs that no one appeared to be actually using at that precise moment. Then, looking like a large, round, furry animal with no head and two legs he left the cave and set off through the snow. A cave of his own was what he was looking for. Not too big. Just somewhere he could roll up in his furs and dream the winter away. It was more difficult than he had imagined. Caves weren't that easily come by, and they all appeared to belong to someone already.

Littlenose was a long way from home when he spied the dark opening of a cave among a pile of boulders. About time, too, he thought. Although it was winter, the noonday sun was warm; particularly to someone laden down with fur bed-clothes. He looked carefully around; there were no signs of a fire or anything else that might suggest people. Cautiously he entered. The cave seemed spacious and had a soft, sandy floor. Might as well give it a try. Littlenose spread out the furs, then lay down and rolled himself up in them. It was perfect. And it seemed such a pity after coming all this way to waste such a find. He would start his hibernation there and then.

Littlenose woke with a start. Was it spring already? He didn't feel as if he had slept for very long. Something hit him gently on the head. He put his hand up to feel. His hair felt wet, and something

hit the back of his hand . . . a drop of water.
Littlenose jumped up. He could hear it now. A
steady drip, drip! He looked up. The sun must be
melting the snow, and the cave had a leaking roof.
No wonder nobody lived here. He gathered up his
bedding before it got too wet, and hurried out into
the open again.

Well, the day was young. Still plenty of time to
find a suitable cave. And only a short distance away,
partly screened by a clump of bare trees, was
another opening in the side of a high bank.

This time, Littlenose was taking no chances. He left his fur covers outside and carefully examined the floor for puddles and damp patches, and peered as well as he was able into the gloom above his head for any sign of a leak. It seemed perfect! The trees outside cut off most of the light from the very back of the cave, but Littlenose groped around and spread the fur rugs and bed covers into a comfortable bed. Then he rolled himself up and closed his eyes to await the coming of spring.

Littlenose woke slowly. He felt quite refreshed. Was it spring already? Well, there was one way to find out. He made to push back the bed-clothes . . . and had a horrible surprise. He couldn't *move!*

Something seemed to be holding his arms tight. He couldn't move his body, although his legs seemed to be free. What had happened? Was it magic? Had he perhaps blundered into a Straightnose cave and they had put a spell on him? He tried again, and found that he could move one hand and arm just a bit. He began to investigate with his fingers. All he could feel was the fur of the bed-clothes. He could recognise each piece by the feel. There was the grey wolf skin with its long, soft fur. And the short soft fur of the cover made from many rabbit skins stitched together. And the tiger skin rug. The red fox. The bear skin. The . . .! Wait a minute!

HE DIDN'T HAVE ANY BEAR SKIN COVERS!

Pulling his fingers away from the bear skin, he
twisted his head as far round as he could, and in the
dim light from the cave entrance, found himself
looking straight into the face of a sleeping bear. A
sleeping bear with one huge, hairy arm around
Littlenose, cuddling him as it slept. Littlenose's
heart almost stopped beating with fright. What had
happened? Had the bear come in after he had gone
to sleep . . . or was it already asleep and hibernating
when Littlenose had made up his bed in the
semi-darkness? It didn't really matter. What
mattered was getting out before the bear woke. It
might wake hungry, and Littlenose didn't fancy
being a midnight snack for a hibernating bear. He
struggled gently to free himself, and the bear
wrapped its arm even tighter around him than
before until he could scarcely breathe.

68

What was he to do? Kick the bear? Perhaps biting the bear might make it let go? On the other hand that was more likely to wake it up – the last thing he wanted to do. Desperately, he racked his brains for something that might make the bear let go but not waken it.

Ah, but there was a way, and it might just work. With the hand which had felt the fur covers, Littlenose reached up under the bear's arm, and tickled it. The bear gave a sort of snort and moved slightly. Again Littlenose tickled, and this time the bear gave a kind of bear giggle in its sleep and wriggled its shoulders. "It's working," thought Littlenose. Again and again he tickled the bear, and each time it relaxed its grip a little, and even had a bear-like smile on its face. One last tickle and the bear humped right over on to its other side, and Littlenose moved just in time to avoid being squashed. He was free! Stealthily he pulled the fur bedding away from beside the sleeping bear. One cover wouldn't come, and he saw that the bear had it in a bundle, cuddling it instead of Littlenose. He decided to leave it.

With his bundle in his arms, Littlenose tip-toed
from the cave, then ran as fast as his legs would
carry him, expecting any moment an angry roar
from the cave. But the bear was sound asleep again
and dreaming bear dreams.

After all the trouble he had had, anyone except
Littlenose would have given up the whole idea of
hibernating and gone home. Littlenose was made of
sterner stuff. As he walked back towards the caves
he thought, "Ready-made caves seem to have
ready-made problems. It would be better if I could
make my own cave. What is a cave, anyway? Only a
pile of rocks with a hole in the middle." Finding
enough rocks might be difficult. But it didn't *need* to
be rocks!

A short distance from the caves where the tribe
lived, he stopped. The snow lay firm and level all
around, and Littlenose began to roll a snowball.
When it was about knee-high he rolled another, and
another, until he was surrounded by large

snowballs. He made a ring of snowballs about
four paces across. Then he built another slightly
smaller ring on top, and another on top of that. He
went on until he had used up all his snowballs and
filled in the gaps with handfuls of snow. It looked
like a big heap of snow, but Littlenose knew that it
was hollow inside like a cave. It was a pity he had
forgotten to make a door, but he managed to drag
one of the bottom snowballs out, and there it was. A
custom-built cave made of snow! He crawled inside
with his bedding. It was quite dry. Why hadn't he
thought of this before? At last, his own hibernating
cave.

Now, while Littlenose had been busy with his
snow cave, another member of the tribe was hard at
work, too. It was Nosey, chief tracker because of his
remarkably handsome and sensitive Neanderthal
nose. Now he came snuffling along, bent almost
double in his winter hunting robe, his famous nose
sticking out from the hood and held a mere

hairsbreadth from the ground. The afternoon sun
was still quite warm, and Nosey mopped his brow
with the back of his hand. "Must be out of
training," he said to himself. "Not only warm, bit
out of puff, even on the level. Must have a rest."

He straightened his back and looked around.
Where was he? What happened? No wonder he was
breathless . . . he had been climbing a hill! But there
shouldn't *be* a hill here, not even a small round-
topped one like this he was standing on. Bit slippery
too, the warm sun was beginning to melt the snow.
Nosey could feel the snow dissolving beneath his
feet, but before he could ponder the mystery further
the whole thing caved in.

Littlenose thought the sky had fallen as Nosey
landed with a soggy thump right on top of him.
They both struggled out of the slushy mess together.
"YOU!" shouted Nosey. "I might have known it
was one of your tricks! Wait till I see your Father,
my lad." And he stalked off, trying to look dignified
with the inside of his robe full of melting snow.

72

But Littlenose paid no attention to Nosey or his threat. A sudden thought had come to him. He knew why people didn't hibernate. They would miss the Sun Dance, the great Neanderthal Midwinter festival! And that would never do. He'd really had a very narrow escape.

Littlenose gathered up his fur bedding and set off for home, wondering what Mother would say when she saw everything sopping wet. And would she believe that one of her best fur rugs had been stolen by a black bear?

Littlenose the Life-saver

Despite its name, the weather during the Ice Age was not just a matter of ice and snow. It rained a lot, more than in the Good Old Days according to the older Neanderthal folk; but, the wind . . . that was something else. The Neanderthal folk lived in caves, which have no doors, so the only protection against cold winds was to get as far into the cave as possible, wear every piece of fur they owned, and huddle over the fire, if the ferocious draughts hadn't blown it out.

However, wind wasn't entirely a bad thing. The fires which warmed the caves and cooked the food also kept wild animals at bay. So, the gathering of fuel was an important part of Neanderthal life. Most of the time it meant trudging off into the woods with a flint axe and laboriously dragging back fallen branches or even more laboriously cutting down a not-too-big tree. But, in the autumn, as the last of the leaves were turning red, there would come a wind fit, you might think, to blow everything off the face of the earth. It didn't, but it blew down a great supply of limbs and branches, and even whole trees. The people would huddle in their caves and listen to the howling of the wind outside. "Ah," they would say wisely to one another, "it's an ill wind that doesn't blow *some* good!"

One morning, after a night of screaming gales, Littlenose set off with his Father and other men of the tribe to gather firewood. Although the wind had died somewhat with the coming of daylight, it was still blowing in strong gusts, and the wood-gatherers bent their heads into it as it tugged at their furs and tried to sweep them off their feet.

But the gale had done a good job. The ground
was strewn with enough fuel to last the whole tribe
for a long time to come. The party made several
trips back to the caves until there was nothing left
worth gathering. Littlenose was weary from the
work, and he hoped that now they could go home.
Then Father pointed to a patch of forest close to the
river and much farther from home. "Let's try
there," he shouted. "There's plenty of daylight left,
and we can't have too much fire wood!" The others
nodded, more or less enthusiastically, and off they
trudged across the open plain towards the distant
trees. Out of the shelter of the forest the wind
pushed them this way and that, completely taking
away Littlenose's breath. Half-way there he
stopped. "Just give me a moment to get my breath
back," he panted.

"Good idea," said one of the men. And they sat
on the ground with their backs to the wind, which
actually seemed to be less strong. In fact, when they

stood up to go on their way they could have sworn
that it was beginning to die away altogether.

The trees were still some way off when Littlenose
pointed. "Look," he said, "we needn't go so far.
There are lots of branches blown from the forest and
lying about in the grass. Why not gather those?"
Why not, indeed, the men agreed, and they
scattered in all directions, picking up tree branches
and piling them in handy piles for carrying home.
And the wind *was* getting less, and a sort of eerie
calm had fallen over the plain. The party were now
well separated from one another, and Littlenose was
working his way along the steep river bank when he
heard a shout. One man was standing waving his
arms and shouting. It sounded like a warning. Was
it a woolly rhinoceros, or a sabre-toothed tiger? He
was pointing to the sky where a great black cloud
had formed against the grey. "He must think it's
going to rain," said Littlenose to himself. "What a
fuss to make about a spot of rain!" Yet it didn't look

like a rain cloud. It was low in the sky, with what looked like a long tail trailing towards the ground.

The man shouted again. Something that sounded like "WHIRLWIND!"

"WHIRL . . . *what*?" thought Littlenose.

Next moment he staggered as a gust of wind nearly bowled him over. There came another, and another, then a roaring in the air that grew louder every moment. The men were by now running in all directions as the strange black cloud rushed down upon them. And Littlenose froze with horror at what he saw. The tail of the cloud was a swiftly spiralling column of wind which sucked up branches, bushes, and even small trees as it advanced over the plain.

Littlenose watched a clump of silver birches suddenly stripped of their leaves, and all but the biggest torn from the ground and carried high into the air, to be scattered moments later smashed and broken on the flattened grass. Almost too late Littlenose began to run. He ran towards the river, while the whirlwind raced behind him, deafening him with its howl, and tugging roughly at his furs. At the last moment he saw a jumble of rocks and dived head first into a deep crevice.

It was like the end of the world. The whirlwind seemed to be trying to drag Littlenose out of his refuge while it showered him with leaves, branches, dirt and small stones.

Then, it had gone; and Littlenose poked his head out from the rocks and watched the whirlwind cross the river in a cloud of mud and water before twisting its way towards the distant hills.

Littlenose climbed up on to the river bank, stood up and looked all around. And saw no one. The wind still blew in occasional strong gusts, and the path of the whirlwind was marked by a wide track of smashed and flattened trees and bushes, as if a huge herd of bison had stampeded. There was no sign of the men. He was alone. He ran out into the plain, and towards the forest. Everyone was gone! Swept away by the whirlwind? It was too awful even to think about. "Probably ran off home," thought Littlenose. "I'd better do the same." But he had only gone a couple of steps when he heard a noise. A human noise. Someone had groaned. He ran back to the river bank, and there by the water's edge lay a figure. It was a man, lying face downward on a tangle of tree branches floating close to the edge. Littlenose waded in and started to drag the man towards the bank. He pulled him on to the shingle and rolled him on to his back. At least he was still breathing . . . but it wasn't his state of health that caught Littlenose's attention. He had thought that it might be one of the wood gatherers . . . but, far from it. The man who lay at his feet fluttering his eye-lids and spitting out water and bits of leaf was a STRAIGHTNOSE! A deadly enemy of the Neanderthal folk. He was tall and slim, with a slender neck and the straight, narrow nose that gave his people their name. Littlenose had one thought. *Run!*

By now the Straightnose had opened his eyes. He sat up, grabbed hold of Littlenose's wrist, and said something in his own language. Hoping for the best, Littlenose smiled as best he could, nodded, and said, "Yes, sir!"

The man frowned, then slowly got to his feet, still holding Littlenose. He seemed to have hurt his leg, and after a few stumbling steps he leaned on Littlenose for support. They made their way up the bank and on to the level plain. Littlenose started to say, "Well, time I was getting home . . ." The Straightnose didn't even pause to listen. Taking an even firmer grip of Littlenose's wrist and leaning even more heavily on his shoulder, he began to limp away from the river and, worse, away from home.

The river was far behind them when at last they stopped. The man let go of Littlenose, who was too weary to even think of trying to run away. In any case he had lost all sense of direction and had no idea where he was. They had stopped by a clump of bushes, and the Straightnose reached under them and drew out a long, dangerous-looking spear. He also drew out a skin pouch with fruit and dried meat in it. He handed some to Littlenose and they sat on the ground to eat.

Littlenose wished the man would stop staring. He
pointed at Littlenose's berry-sized nose, touched his
own, and said something in his own language.
Again, Littlenose hopefully replied, "Yes, sir!" and
smiled. He thought the man smiled slightly, too,
and kept on staring at him until he suddenly pulled
himself to his feet, and Littlenose with him. When
next he spoke, Littlenose knew exactly what he
meant, and he picked up the food pouch and heaved
it on to his shoulder. The Straightnose no longer
held his wrist, but made Littlenose walk in front
while he leaned on his spear for support instead of
Littlenose's shoulder.

The sun was well down in the sky when they next stopped to rest. The Straightnose man's pace had been getting steadily slower, which suited Littlenose, as the food pouch seemed to be getting steadily heavier. The Straightnose pointed in the direction of the setting sun and said something, then laid down the spear and stretched out on the grass for a nap, indicating by gestures that he thought Littlenose should do the same. Littlenose didn't lie down, but he sat with his back to a handy tree stump and wondered if he would ever see home again. Perhaps he should get some sleep. His head nodded as he watched swaying grass heads against the sunset. Was something wrong? Grass heads swayed in the wind, but since the whirlwind there had not been a breath of wind. He stood up and peered into the growing dusk. The grass was still for a moment, then it swayed and parted as, barely twenty paces away, a large, hungry-looking hyena

stepped into a clear patch.

Littlenose gasped and jumped back in fright, falling over the Straightnose's injured leg. The man grabbed him and shouted as he sat up. He shouted again, and had started to shake Littlenose when the hyena gave a low, chuckling cry, partly in surprise at the sound of a human voice, and partly in anticipation of a good evening meal. The man pushed Littlenose to one side and picked up his spear and, with only a moment's aim, threw it at the hyena. But, his bad leg gave way as he threw, and the spear flew over the animal's head and stuck in the ground. There was nothing left to do now but run, and Littlenose did just that. Then he stopped, and looked back. The Straightnose was trying to follow him, but could only manage to hobble slowly, while the hyena steadily advanced, shoulders hunched, teeth gleaming, and giggling in its own unpleasant hyena way.

This could be Littlenose's chance. He could escape while his captor was busy with the hyena. That is, while the Straightnose was being eaten. Yet people only survived in the Ice Age by banding together to protect each other, and even Straightnoses were people!

Without another thought, Littlenose turned. He had no plan, but he had not saved the man from drowning just to feed a hungry hyena! The hyena had forgotten Littlenose, and now it was crouched,

winding up for the final rush at his victim. It took
one step . . . and yelped as a large stone hit it on the
ear. It looked round and another stone bounced off
its nose, followed by one in the eye. This was unfair!
Hyenas preyed on old, sick or injured victims, and
here was an injured victim ripe for preying on.
There was nothing in hyena rules about non-injured
victims who threw stones! Whimpering, it pawed its
bloody nose, and as another stone smacked it in the
ribs it turned and loped off swiftly into the gathering
night.

Littlenose walked back to the man, who held out

his hand before retrieving the spear and signalling
Littlenose to follow him with the food pouch. Their
resumed march didn't last long. A bright glow
appeared in the sky, and from the top of a ridge
Littlenose found himself looking down on a large
Straightnose encampment. It was just as he had
feared. He was going to be paraded as a prisoner . . .
and more than likely eaten if half the stories about
the Straightnoses were true! He had fallen into
Straightnose hands once before, and had been
extremely lucky to have escaped.

As they passed between the tents, a crowd of

curious Straightnoses followed. Some Straightnose boys shouted at Littlenose, and one prodded him with a stick, but they backed off when his captor waved his spear and shouted back in their own language. A few more steps and they stood beside a fire while the whole Straightnose tribe gathered in a circle. Then the circle parted and a splendid figure approached, and beckoned to Littlenose. It was the Chief, dressed in a long white fur cloak and with feathers in his hair. He said something to Littlenose, who didn't understand, then turned to the man who had brought Littlenose.

And the man began to relate his adventure. He didn't just speak, but mimed and gestured and even broke into a dance at one point, so that Littlenose found that he could follow the story quite well. The man told how he had been out looking for game when he spotted the Neanderthal wood-gathering party. He had climbed a tree to have a better look when the whirlwind came and carried him with the branches he was clinging to into the river. He knew no more until Littlenose had pulled him out and helped him to walk and carry his equipment. And then (the man paused for dramatic effect), and then they had been attacked by the most ferocious hyena you could imagine – and this fearless Neanderthal boy had driven it off! At this the crowd went mad, clapping, shouting, cheering, until the Chief held up his hand.

There followed a long discussion between the Chief and the Straightnose men, no doubt about what was to be done with Littlenose. Not eaten, that was certain. The Chief had been looking closely at Littlenose for some moments, and when next he spoke, Littlenose was sure he caught the word "Redhead". Yes, there it was again. Boldly, Littlenose spoke up, "I have an Uncle Redhead. He has many Straightnose friends." At the mention of Uncle Redhead, the Chief and his men smiled, the rest of the people laughed . . . and one pretty Straightnose girl blushed. After that, everything seemed to happen at once. Food and drink were produced, and people came up and spoke to Littlenose as he ate. Everyone seemed to want to talk about Uncle Redhead, although what they said Littlenose hadn't the faintest idea. The pretty girl showed him a picture of a beaver drawn on birch bark just like the one Uncle Redhead had made for Littlenose.

90

Then it was time to go. Littlenose was lifted on to the shoulders of a Straightnose hunter, and other hunters gathered around him. Everyone said a Straightnose "goodbye" while they shook his hand or patted his head. The pretty girl blew a kiss and said, "Redhead!" before disappearing into the crowd. The last goodbyes were said, and Littlenose was on his way home. The Straightnoses ran like the wind, taking it in turns to carry Littlenose, and just as dawn was breaking they came to the place where Littlenose had last seen his own people before the whirlwind came. The Straightnoses put him on the ground, shook his hand again, and were gone.

"What an adventure!" he thought. "Just wait until I tell them what nice people the Straightnoses really are. Not in the least evil monsters that eat Neanderthal children." Then he paused. Who was going to believe him? Certainly not Father. Nothing would ever shake his fixed Neanderthal ideas about the Straightnoses . . . and everything else for that matter.

Ah, but what about Uncle Redhead? He would believe him all right . . . particularly the bit about the pretty Straightnose girl.

He'd tell the others that he had been blown by the whirlwind over the hills and far away, and had been all night walking home. All he wanted to do now was to reach the family cave as quickly as possible and curl up in bed in his own special corner.

Was the Ice Age dangerous?

So, Littlenose survived more adventures to return home safely to Father, Mother and Two-Eyes. It's surprising that he *had* so many adventures, because usually each one looked like being his last. He fell into rivers and out of trees. He was chased by enraged woolly rhinoceroses and hunted by hungry sabre-toothed tigers. Mother was angry when he came home late, but she must have been quite surprised that he came home at all sometimes!

Things are much safer nowadays . . . unless, of course, you count people who are knocked down by buses; or people who fall down stairs and off bicycles. And Littlenose never scraped his knees falling on roller skates. *And*, modern boys and girls fall out of trees and into rivers just as easily as he did. We certainly aren't chased by enraged taxis or hunted for food by hungry buses, but we still have to be every bit as careful making our way through the streets to the shops as the Neanderthal folk had to be when they went into the forest to hunt.

Perhaps, after all, today is just as dangerous to us as the Ice Age was to Littlenose. Do *you* think so?

1OO,OOO YEARS AGO people wore no clothes. They lived in caves and hunted animals for food. They were called NEANDERTHAL.

50,OOO YEARS AGO when Littlenose lived, clothes were made out of fur. But now there were other people. Littlenose called them Straightnoses. Their proper name is HOMO SAPIENS.

5,OOO YEARS AGO there were no Neanderthal people left. People wore cloth as well as fur. They built in wood and stone. They grew crops and kept cattle.

1,OOO YEARS AGO towns were built, and men began to travel far from home by land and sea to explore the world.

5OO YEARS AGO towns became larger, as did the ships in which men travelled. The houses they built were very like those we see today.

1OO YEARS AGO people used machines to do a lot of the harder work. They could now travel by steam train. Towns and cities became very big, with factories as well as houses.

TODAY we don't hunt for our food, but buy it in shops. We travel by car and aeroplane. Littlenose would not understand any of this. Would YOU like to live as Littlenose did?